EAU CLAIRE DISTRICT LIBRARY
6528 East Main Street
P.O. Box 328
EAU CLAIRE, MI 49111

W9-AJT-101

Lun

GIFTS FROM THE GODS

To Ann, muse of children's literature

— L.L.L.

For Alison—in this book and in life,

my goddess, my nymph, my Muse, my Fortune.

—G.H.

Text copyright © 2011 by Lise Lunge-Larsen
Illustrations copyright © 2011 by Gareth Hinds
All rights reserved. For information about permission to reproduce selections from this book,
write to Permissions, Houghton Mifflin Harcourt Publishing Company,
215 Park Avenue South, New York, New York 10003.
Houghton Mifflin Books for Children is an imprint of Houghton Mifflin Harcourt Publishing Company.
www.hmhbooks.com

The text of this book is set in Minion Pro.
The illustrations are pencil and watercolor with Photoshop.

Library of Congress Cataloging-in-Publication Data
Lunge-Larsen, Lise.
Gifts from the gods: ancient words and wisdom from Greek and Roman mythology / written by Lise Lunge-Larsen ;
illustrated by Gareth Hinds.
p. cm.
ISBN 978-0-547-15229-5
1. Vocabulary—Juvenile literature. 2. Mythology—Juvenile literature. I. Hinds, Gareth, 1971– II. Title.
PE1449.L74 2011
401'.4—dc22
2010031635

Manufactured in China
LEO 10 9 8 7 6 5 4 3 2

4500324799

Definitions and pronounciations copyright © 2010 by Houghton Mifflin Harcourt Publishing Company, adapted and
reproduced by permission from *The American Heritage Dictionary of the English Language,* fourth edition.

GIFTS FROM THE GODS

Ancient Words & Wisdom from Greek & Roman Mythology

by LISE LUNGE-LARSEN   Illustrated by GARETH HINDS

HOUGHTON MIFFLIN BOOKS FOR CHILDREN

HOUGHTON MIFFLIN HARCOURT

BOSTON   NEW YORK

EAU CLAIRE DISTRICT LIBRARY

T 152252

Humans have always loved telling stories, and to tell them we use words.

Sometimes, however, the words themselves have stories to tell. The ancient words in this book come from the gods, goddesses, heroes, and humans in Greek and Roman mythology. The stories of their adventures so captured people's imagination that they have been told and retold for thousands of years, and their names have survived as words we use every day. Not only do these tales illuminate and explain words, but they also help us understand our own world more deeply.

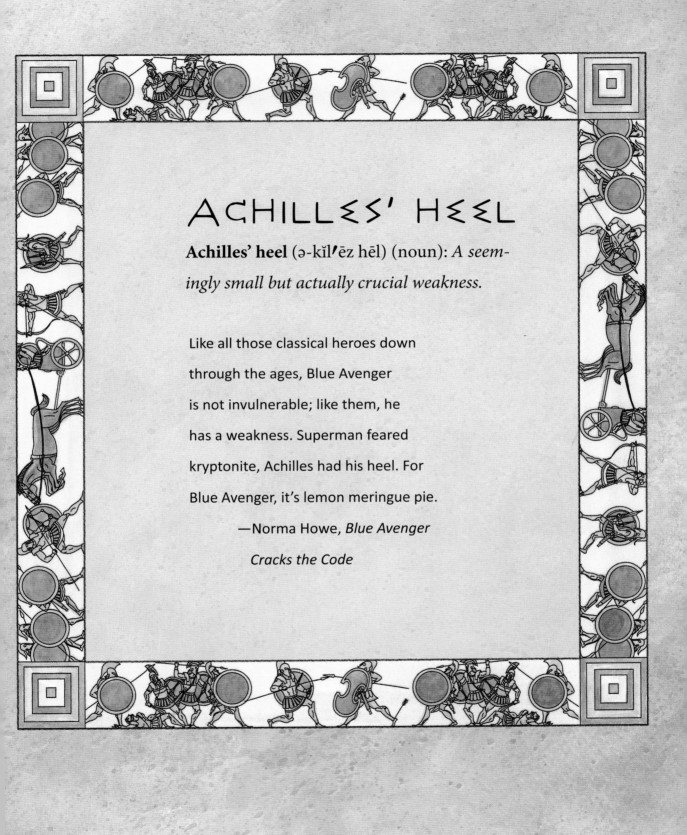

ACHILLES' HEEL

Achilles' heel (ə-kĭl′ēz hēl) (noun): *A seemingly small but actually crucial weakness.*

Like all those classical heroes down

through the ages, Blue Avenger

is not invulnerable; like them, he

has a weakness. Superman feared

kryptonite, Achilles had his heel. For

Blue Avenger, it's lemon meringue pie.

—Norma Howe, *Blue Avenger*

Cracks the Code

W hen **Achilles** was born, his mother wrapped her arms around her little son and decided she didn't ever want him to die. And because she was no ordinary mortal, but a nymph, she knew how to fulfill her wish.

She carried baby Achilles all the way to the river Styx, which separates the land of the living from the land of the dead. There she immersed him in its sacred water, grasping his heel so tightly that it didn't get wet.

As he grew, Achilles excelled beyond all ordinary humans. He ran faster than a horse, fought tirelessly for hours, and wielded a sword with such skill and ferocity that in battle he drove entire armies away all by himself. No arrow, sword, or ax could hurt him—as long as his heel remained untouched.

But when the Battle of Troy broke out and Achilles went to fight, the very thing his mother had tried to prevent happened: during a siege on the city, one fateful arrow pierced his heel, his only mortal part, killing him.

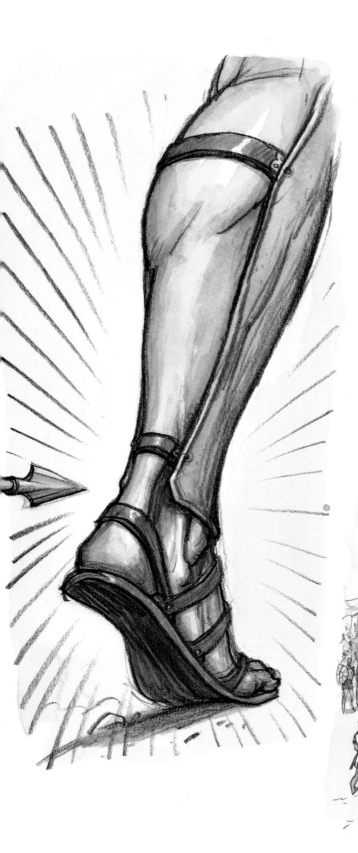

Still, Achilles became revered as one of the greatest of the Greek heroes, for without him, the Greeks would never have defeated the Trojans. He lives on in our language also. We call a person's weakness his or her *Achilles' heel*, especially if that person seems otherwise invincible.

Gods and mortals often spent time with one another and even had children together. Like Achilles, these children sometimes grew up to become so strong and courageous that they seemed like gods. To distinguish them from ordinary humans, the Greeks called these superhumans **heroes,** meaning "defenders and protectors." We use the word in much the same way today.

Achilles' mother was a kind of immortal called a **nymph,** which is a nature goddess. They were lovely maidens who presided over places in nature. There were freshwater nymphs and sea nymphs, mountain nymphs and tree nymphs. All loved to play, bathe, sing, and dance. They also stayed young forever. Immature insects are called **nymphs** after these nature goddesses.

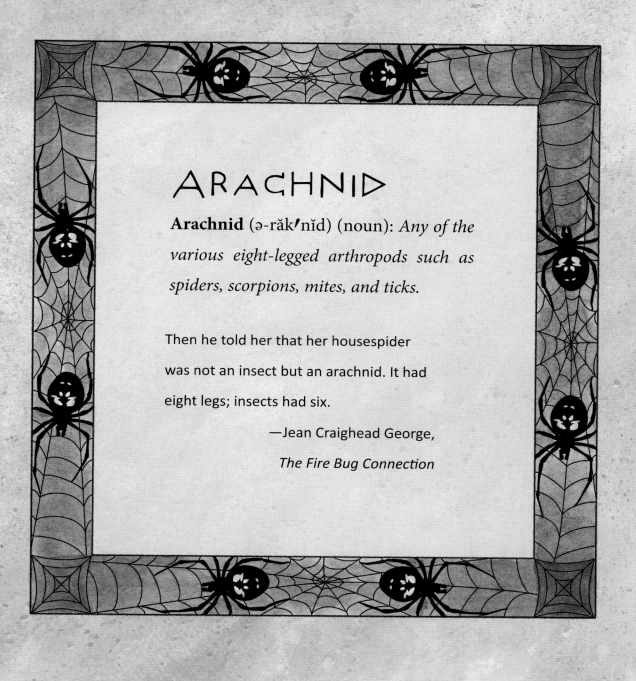

ARACHNID

Arachnid (ə-răk′nĭd) (noun): *Any of the various eight-legged arthropods such as spiders, scorpions, mites, and ticks.*

Then he told her that her housespider was not an insect but an arachnid. It had eight legs; insects had six.

—Jean Craighead George,

The Fire Bug Connection

There once lived a girl named **Arachne** who had learned weaving from Athena, the goddess of the arts. Arachne had become such a clever weaver that people came from miles around to watch her work.

"The gods have given you extraordinary talent," her friends told her.

"The gods have nothing to do with it. My talent is all my own," boasted Arachne.

"You'd better not speak so loudly," warned her friends. "What if Athena hears you?"

I DON'T CARE WHO HEARS ME. I'M THE BEST THERE IS, EVEN BETTER THAN ATHENA.

Suddenly there was a flash of golden light and Athena appeared in the room.

Arachne smiled, sat down at her loom, and said, "Very well, a contest then, to see who is the best in the world."

YOU VAIN, BOASTFUL GIRL!

SINCE YOU ARE SO SURE OF YOURSELF, LET US SEE WHO IS THE BEST WEAVER.

The goddess Athena began weaving a tapestry of Mount Olympus. All the gods were in it—heroic, clever, and handsome. She also wove in all the creatures of creation, and the animals were so lifelike that they seemed to move and breathe.

Arachne also wove a picture of the gods, but it was insulting, showing the gods as lazy, squabbling, boastful, and vain.

Yet Arachne's tapestry was superb. Every knot was perfect and the colors sparkled. Still, when Athena saw the picture, she became furious.

YOUR SKILL IS MATCHLESS, BUT YOUR PRIDE IS UNFORGIVEABLE! HOW DARE YOU SHAME THE GODS?!

Then she struck Arachne with her shuttle. At once Arachne's body began to shrink and shrink until it was a small black blob with spindly legs. Out of her body came a long, thin thread. Arachne had become a spider.

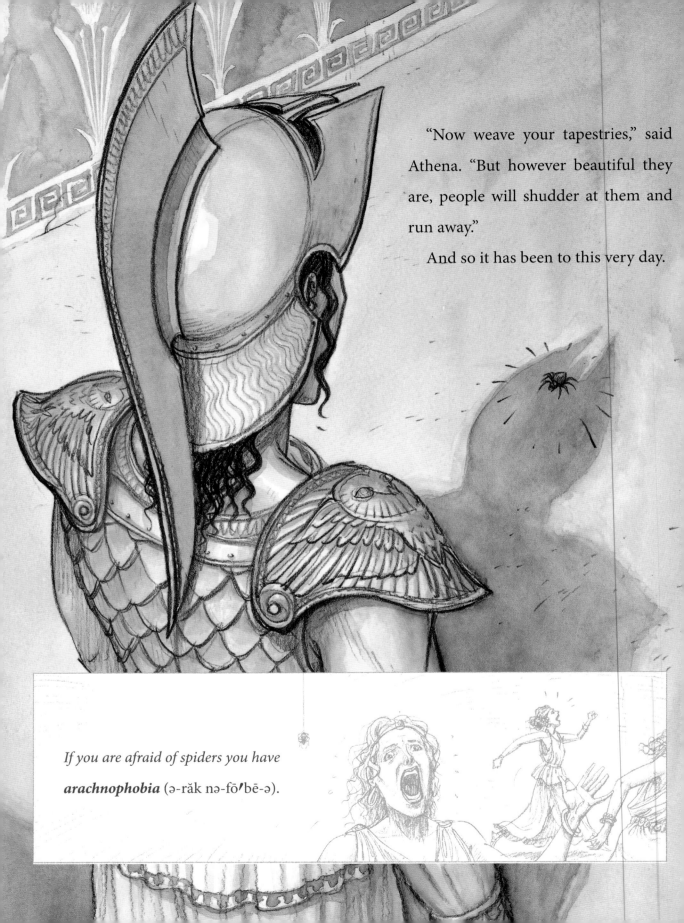

"Now weave your tapestries," said Athena. "But however beautiful they are, people will shudder at them and run away."

And so it has been to this very day.

If you are afraid of spiders you have

arachnophobia (ə-răk nə-fō′bē-ə).

ΣCHO⊙

Echo (ĕk′ō) (noun): *Repetition of a sound by reflection of sound waves from a surface.*

He raised the horn to his lips. The notes sprang loud and clear and even before the signal faded, the wind caught them and seemed to fling the call through all the valley, where it returned in echo after echo.

—Lloyd Alexander, *Taran Wanderer*

Like all wood nymphs, **Echo** was lovely and playful, but she was far too talkative. And she always had to have the last word.

One day as she sat combing her hair by a grove of trees, Hera, the queen of the gods, arrived in search of Zeus, her husband. Zeus, the mightiest god of all, had disappeared from their home on Mount Olympus and Hera was certain that he was in the woods flirting with nymphs. That was, in fact, exactly what Zeus was doing, and Echo, who knew how severely Hera punished anyone who caught Zeus's fancy, at once decided to help her friends the only way she could. Bowing deeply to the queen, Echo began to talk and talk.

She talked so much and for so long that when Hera finally took her leave,
Zeus and the nymphs had fled from the forest.

Furious, Hera turned on Echo.

EAU CLAIRE DISTRICT LIBRARY

Echo wandered about miserably for weeks until one day she spotted a shepherd boy named Narcissus. He was as handsome as a god—tall, broad-shouldered, and with hair the color of sunshine. Echo could not take her eyes off him. She began to follow him everywhere, hoping to catch his attention. But Narcissus never even nodded a greeting.

One day, he strolled into the woods while Echo trailed silently behind. In the afternoon, he came upon a pool of water and bent down for a drink. As he leaned over the smooth dark surface, he caught sight of the most handsome face he had ever seen. Captivated, Narcissus knelt down. He smiled and the youth in the pool smiled back. "I think I love you," said Narcissus.

"Love you," repeated Echo happily.

Too absorbed by the face in the pool to notice her, Narcissus waved his hand in greeting and the youth in the pool waved in return.

Narcissus fell so deeply in love with his own image that he just sat by the pool, gazing at his own beautiful face, forgetting to eat and drink, until finally he pined away and died.

As the gods carried him to the realm of the dead, a new flower sprang up in the place where he had knelt. It is called *narcissus*, better known today as the daffodil, and it is as bright yellow as the hair of the youth who fell in love with himself.

When Narcissus was taken to the underworld, Echo also wasted away until only her voice was left, which to this day you can hear repeating the words of others.

People who spend hours admiring themselves in the mirror, who talk about themselves all the time, and who are interested only in themselves are called **narcissists** *(när′sĭ-sĭsts) after the young man in this story.*

Some individuals are so excessively self-absorbed that it becomes an illness called **narcissism** *(när′sĭ-sĭz′əm).*

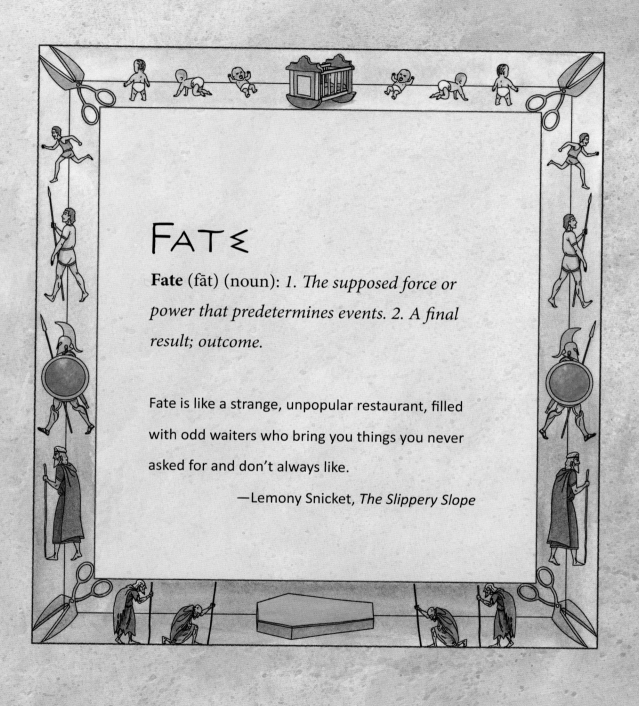

FATE

Fate (fāt) (noun): *1. The supposed force or power that predetermines events. 2. A final result; outcome.*

Fate is like a strange, unpopular restaurant, filled with odd waiters who bring you things you never asked for and don't always like.

—Lemony Snicket, *The Slippery Slope*

The **Fates** were three sisters. These immensely powerful goddesses determined the destiny of every human being. When a pregnant woman went into labor, the Fates watched and waited. As the time of birth drew closer, Clotho, the youngest, spun a thread on her distaff that symbolized the life of the new person. This thread of life was called the stamen, and Clotho spun many different kinds. Some stamen were made of fine linen, and others were made of ordinary wool. Some were fragile and some were tough; some were soft and some were coarse.

While Clotho spun, the middle sister, Lachesis, decided if the new baby's life would be good or bad, blessed with wealth or rife with poverty, orderly or chaotic. The oldest sister, Atropos, cut the thread of life with sharp scissors, determining how long a person would live. Sometimes Clotho spun a thread so sturdy that Atropos had a hard time cutting it. People with such a thread were said to have a strong *stamina* and were blessed with good health all their days.

Once the Fates had made up their minds about a human's destiny, it was impossible to change the outcome. But this didn't stop brides in the city of Athens from trying to influence the future. On their wedding day many young women cut off thick locks of their hair and offered them to the three mighty goddesses in the hope that they would choose a favorable fate for their unborn children.

This Greek belief that the three Fates had power over much of our destiny is the reason we say it is *fate* when things happen that we cannot control.

21

*People who have tremendous physical power and endurance seem to have a strong thread of life. That's why we say these people have great **stamina** (stăm′ə-nə). The thread of life also gave its name to the pollen-producing reproductive part of a flower, called the **stamen** (stā′mən).*

*The Romans named Atropos, the goddess who cut the thread of life, Morta. Her name means "death" and lives on in **mortal** and **mortality,** words we use about things that one day will die. The gods, who will never die, are **immortal.***

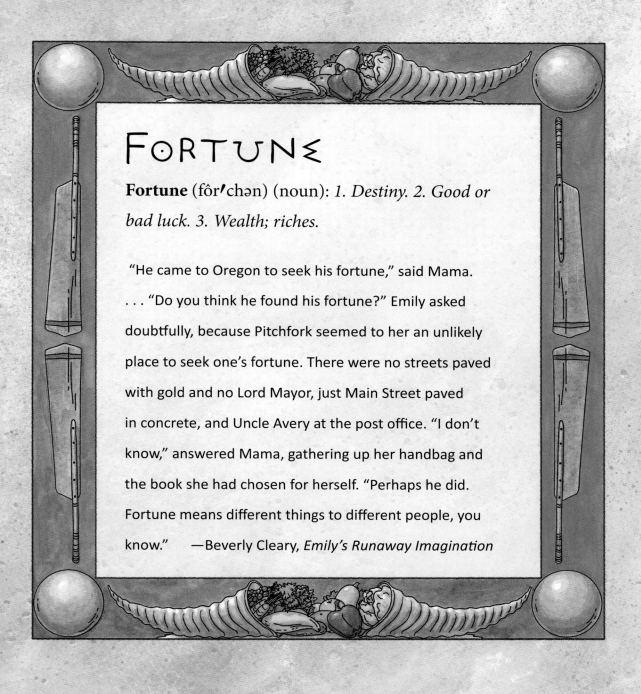

FORTUNE

Fortune (fôr′chən) (noun): *1. Destiny. 2. Good or bad luck. 3. Wealth; riches.*

"He came to Oregon to seek his fortune," said Mama. . . . "Do you think he found his fortune?" Emily asked doubtfully, because Pitchfork seemed to her an unlikely place to seek one's fortune. There were no streets paved with gold and no Lord Mayor, just Main Street paved in concrete, and Uncle Avery at the post office. "I don't know," answered Mama, gathering up her handbag and the book she had chosen for herself. "Perhaps he did. Fortune means different things to different people, you know." —Beverly Cleary, *Emily's Runaway Imagination*

Fortuna was the goddess of luck. She often traveled around on earth and if people caught a glimpse of her they could tell what kind of fortune she brought. If she appeared holding a ship's rudder, it meant she was guiding and conducting the affairs of the world. If she carried a ball, it meant she was concerned with luck, which like a rolling ball can go in any direction. And if she appeared carrying a horn, known as "the horn of plenty," it meant she would bless those she visited with all the abundance and riches of the earth.

Soldiers, sailors, farmers, and all who depended on luck as well as skill constantly prayed to Fortuna, hoping she would favor them. But in truth, she was a fickle goddess. Sometimes she showered people with her attention and their fortunes would rise. Other times she paid no heed at all and allowed terrible accidents to occur. Once, she snatched a sleeping shepherd boy away from a deep well, saving his life. Another time she ignored the pleas of desperate sailors and let their ships sink. She might smile on a man one day yet frown on him the next. The only thing for certain was that she always favored the bold and the brave.

One Roman named Lucius Cornelius Sulla was such a man. Not only was he a courageous fighter on the battlefield, but he was also a daring risk taker. Dressed in clever disguises, he would sneak into the enemy's camp, live among them for days, and gather valuable information. Watching this fearless man always made Fortuna smile.

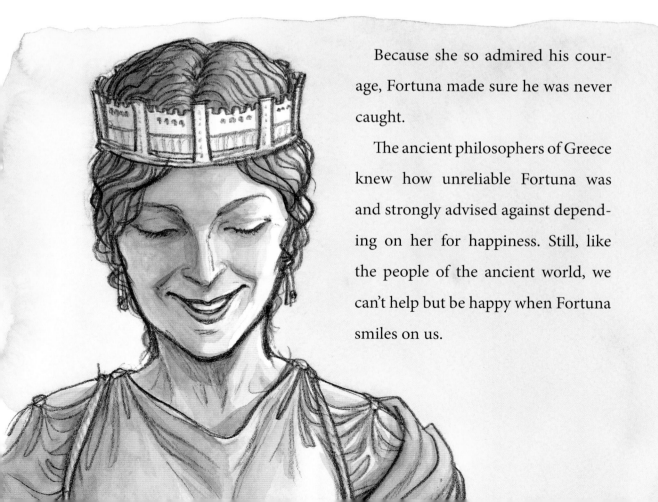

Because she so admired his courage, Fortuna made sure he was never caught.

The ancient philosophers of Greece knew how unreliable Fortuna was and strongly advised against depending on her for happiness. Still, like the people of the ancient world, we can't help but be happy when Fortuna smiles on us.

The "horn of plenty" that Fortuna sometimes carried belonged to a fairy goat named Amaltheia. A never-ending supply of the most delicious food and drink dripped from this magical horn, and Zeus, the chief of the gods, drank from it when he was a baby. The Romans called the horn of plenty a **cornucopia** (kôr′nə-kō′pē-ə). This word now means an abundance of things or a cone-shaped basket overflowing with delectable foods. **Cornucopias** are common at Thanksgiving, when we remember and give thanks for the earth's bounty.

FURY

Fury (fyŏŏr′ē) (noun): *Violent anger; rage.*

We must both have cried out aloud when our eyes met; but while mine was the shrill cry of terror, his was the roar of fury, like a charging bull's.

—Robert Louis Stevenson, *Treasure Island*

The **Furies** were three goddesses of vengeance. Wearing long black robes fastened around the waist with snakes, they hounded lawbreakers, especially murderers. Serpents twined through their long white hair and coiled around their arms. Blood dripped from their black eyes.

They lived in Tartarus, the deepest, darkest part of the underworld, where they persecuted evildoers even after death But they came up to

earth if they were summoned to deal with an injustice.

When the two daughters of a human named Skedasos were brutally killed, he pounded the ground with his fists, calling to the Furies below for vengeance.

Hearing the cries of the grief-struck father, the Furies lifted their heads and listened. Then, seizing their whips, they flew out of the underworld and emerged through cracks and fissures in the craggy mountains. As soon as they caught the scent of the murderers, they gave chase.

The men, seeing the dark, flapping shapes approaching, ran in terror. But they could not escape. Calling down curses, the Furies lashed their whips till the murderers bled. They tore

snakes out from their hair and hurled them at the killers' backs. Down the snakes slid, winding, twisting, but never biting their victims. Instead, they exhaled poisonous fumes that affected the men's minds, and the men began to rave. Refusing to give them any rest, the Furies chased and tormented the murderers until at last they went mad.

Such was the punishment of the Furies.

Even though the Furies existed to avenge evil, all people, good and bad, were scared of these goddesses, for who among us has never done anything wrong?

When someone makes you mad, they **infuriate** you, and when you are filled with anger, you are **furious**. Also, when anger overcomes a group of people, they are collectively in a **furor**.

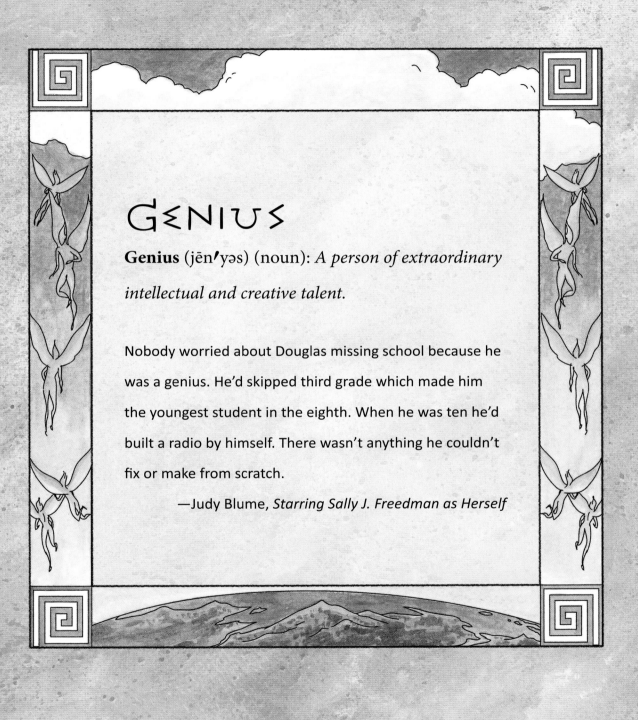

GENIUS

Genius (jēn′yəs) (noun): *A person of extraordinary intellectual and creative talent.*

Nobody worried about Douglas missing school because he was a genius. He'd skipped third grade which made him the youngest student in the eighth. When he was ten he'd built a radio by himself. There wasn't anything he couldn't fix or make from scratch.

—Judy Blume, *Starring Sally J. Freedman as Herself*

The Romans adopted all the Greek gods as their own, but they also had many gods that were unique to them. In fact, the Romans had minor gods in charge of almost everything in their lives. There were gods for a baby's first tooth, for the pots in the kitchen, for bread baking, for bees, and for door handles.

The Romans also believed that each and every human being had a personal spirit, called a **Genius,** which was assigned at birth. Your Genius made you different from other people. It determined your character, oversaw your work, and finally brought you out of this world at death.

Working tirelessly on your behalf, your Genius carried your prayers and wishes to the gods, making sure they were heard. In fact, the ancients believed that the air was filled with thousands and thousands of invisible Genii that brought messages back and forth between humans and gods.

Most Genii were kind, helpful, and protective. But once in a while a Genius could manifest itself in another way—as an evil spirit that caused you to do bad things.

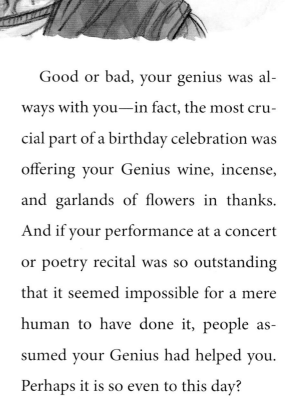

Good or bad, your genius was always with you—in fact, the most crucial part of a birthday celebration was offering your Genius wine, incense, and garlands of flowers in thanks. And if your performance at a concert or poetry recital was so outstanding that it seemed impossible for a mere human to have done it, people assumed your Genius had helped you. Perhaps it is so even to this day?

The Greeks called this
personal spirit your
daemon (dī′mōn).
A daemon had exactly
the same function and
meaning as a Genius, but
it became our word for an
evil spirit, a **demon.**

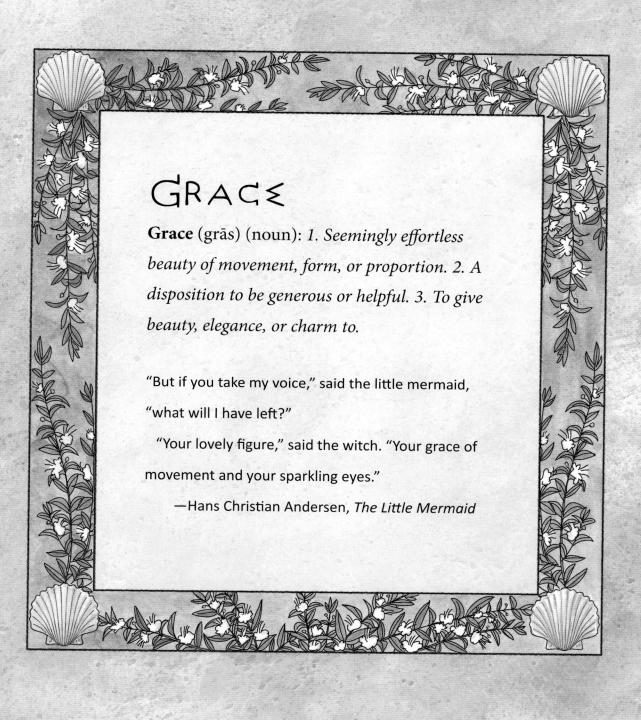

GRACE

Grace (grās) (noun): *1. Seemingly effortless beauty of movement, form, or proportion. 2. A disposition to be generous or helpful. 3. To give beauty, elegance, or charm to.*

"But if you take my voice," said the little mermaid, "what will I have left?"

"Your lovely figure," said the witch. "Your grace of movement and your sparkling eyes."

—Hans Christian Andersen, *The Little Mermaid*

The three goddesses called the **Graces** were always invited to festivals and celebrations. Whenever they arrived, heroes stopped boasting, poets recited with greater eloquence, musicians played more passionately, and philosophers spoke with deeper wisdom.

Elegant and charming, the Graces radiated generosity, beauty, and joy. Wreaths of sweet-smelling myrtle encircled their thick, glossy hair, gossamer gowns floated around their bodies, and their dark eyes sparkled with pleasure. Yet nobody was jealous of them, for their presence enhanced everyone else's beauty.

Nor were the Graces ever jealous. When the goddess of beauty and love, named Venus, arrived from the sea, the Graces ran down to the shore to welcome her. Before they allowed anyone else to see Venus, they rubbed her body with scented ointments and clothed her with silken garments. On her head they placed a finely wrought crown of gold. Then, satisfied that she could not be made lovelier, they brought her to Mount Olympus, where the other gods greeted her.

From that day on, Venus, like many other goddesses, became so fond of the Graces that she asked them to attend her as often as possible. It is no wonder their name came to mean all things charming and elegant.

*The name "the Graces" for these goddesses comes to us via Old French. Their Latin name is **Gratia**. Because **gratia** (grä′tē-ä) means both pleasing and thankful, the sweet helpfulness of these goddesses survives not just in a host of words such as **graceful** and **gracious,** but also in several words that express thankfulness, such as **grateful** and **gratitude.***

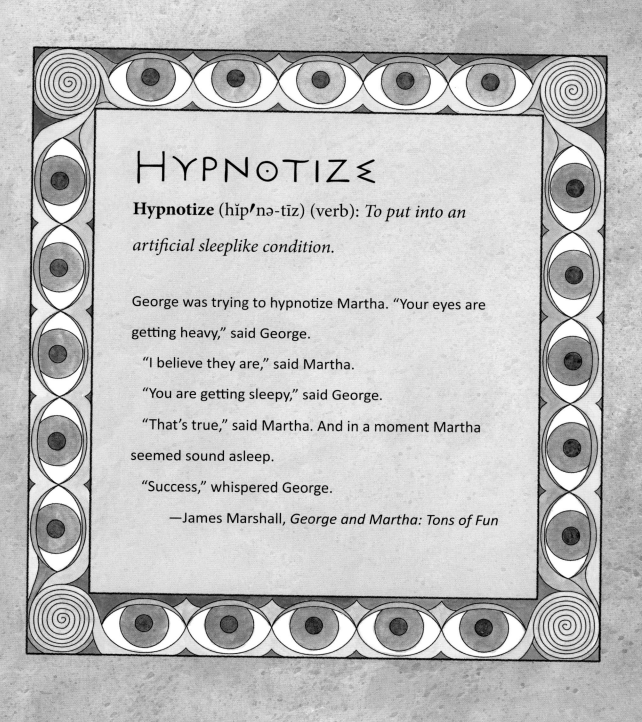

HYPNOTIZE

Hypnotize (hĭp′nə-tīz) (verb): *To put into an artificial sleeplike condition.*

George was trying to hypnotize Martha. "Your eyes are getting heavy," said George.

"I believe they are," said Martha.

"You are getting sleepy," said George.

"That's true," said Martha. And in a moment Martha seemed sound asleep.

"Success," whispered George.

—James Marshall, *George and Martha: Tons of Fun*

Hypnos, the god of sleep, was a great deal more powerful than his soft, droopy eyes suggested. He could put anyone to sleep whenever he wanted. He would doze all day and rise only in the evening when his mother, Nyx, the goddess of the night, roused him. Then he climbed onto the train of her dark, starry dress and together they floated across the sky. Sitting at the edge of his mother's long, billowing gown, Hypnos slowly poured sleep out of an enormous clay vessel. When everyone on earth was fast asleep, he returned home and went straight back to bed to nap some more.

The gods and goddesses often played tricks on one another, and to avoid getting caught, they asked for Hypnos's help. During the Trojan War, Zeus, the chief of the gods, and Hera, his wife, supported opposite sides. As long as Zeus was helping the Trojans, the Greeks had no chance of winning. Hera decided Zeus must be distracted from the battle—and what is better distraction than sleep?

At first, Hypnos was reluctant to help, fearful of Zeus's wrath. But then Hera made him an offer:

IF YOU PUT ZEUS TO SLEEP, I WILL GIVE YOU THALIA, THE YOUNGEST OF THE GRACES, FOR YOUR WIFE.

Hypnos had been in love with Thalia forever, and he immediately agreed to help. He flew to a grove of tall pines from which he could see Zeus resting below. Clothing himself in mist, Hypnos climbed the highest tree and upon reaching the top, he hid among the branches. When he was certain that Zeus did not suspect his presence, he sprinkled sleep onto the mighty god. At once Zeus's eyes closed and he was in a deep slumber.

While Zeus slept, Hera helped her heroes in battle. When Zeus finally woke and saw the Trojan army fleeing from the Greeks, he right away understood the trick Hera and Hypnos had played on him. He became so angry that he chased Hypnos up and down the heavens, over mountains, through woods and valleys, and all the way into the underworld. Finally, Hypnos hid underneath his mother's gown, avoiding Zeus's wrath because of her protection. Even Zeus had no power over the goddess of the night.

Hypnos's name lives on today. When somebody is put into an artificial sleep or trance, as Zeus was, we call it being *hypnotized*.

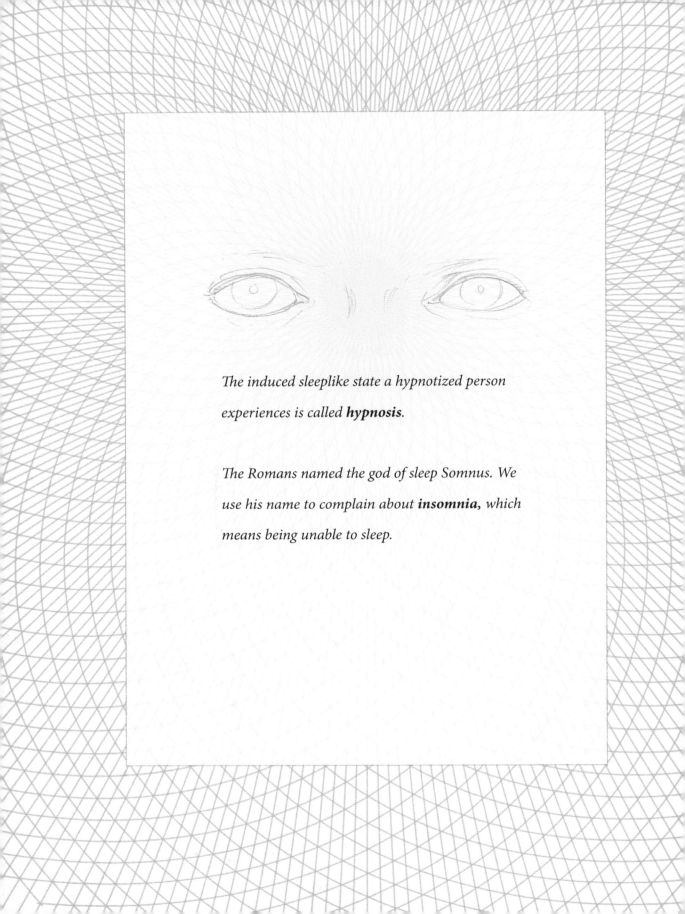

The induced sleeplike state a hypnotized person experiences is called **hypnosis**.

The Romans named the god of sleep Somnus. We use his name to complain about **insomnia,** which means being unable to sleep.

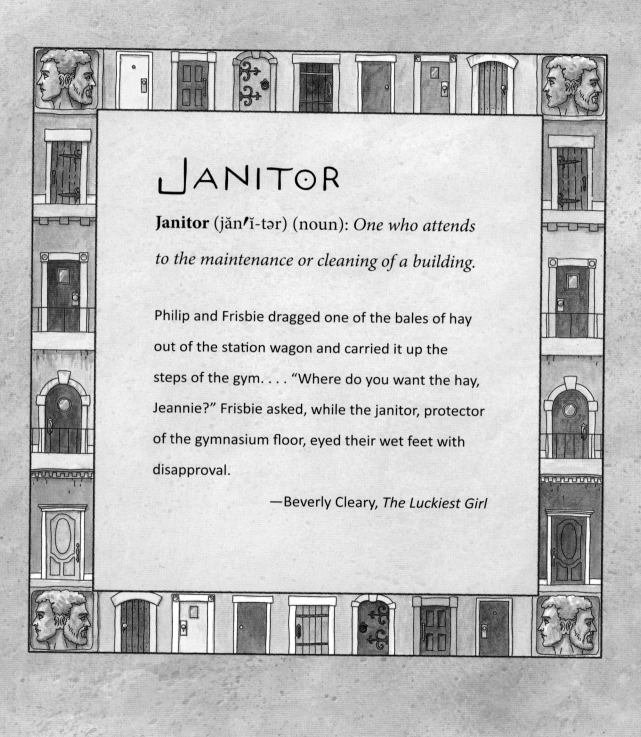

JANITOR

Janitor (jăn′ĭ-tər) (noun): *One who attends to the maintenance or cleaning of a building.*

Philip and Frisbie dragged one of the bales of hay out of the station wagon and carried it up the steps of the gym. . . . "Where do you want the hay, Jeannie?" Frisbie asked, while the janitor, protector of the gymnasium floor, eyed their wet feet with disapproval.

—Beverly Cleary, *The Luckiest Girl*

anus was the god of doorways and hallways, bridges and gates, beginnings and endings. He had two faces: one that looked forward and one that looked backward so that he could see in two directions at once.

The Romans revered Janus for his strength and loyalty. Once, when Janus witnessed an army trying to kidnap a group of innocent women, he became so enraged that he made a volcanic hot spring erupt, burying the attackers and saving the women.

In gratitude for this and for the many ways he looked after them, the Romans carved Janus's likeness on the top of nearly every city gate, allowing him to watch over the citizens inside *and* to keep a sharp lookout for approaching enemies.

The Romans also built an enormous temple in his honor. It ran from east to west, with a door at each end and a statue of Janus in the middle. The doors of this temple were kept open when Rome was at war so that Janus could keep an eye out for enemies. The Romans fought so often that these doors were closed only three times in the first seven hundred years of the city's existence.

While we don't carve Janus's face on buildings, his spirit lives on in the word *janitor,* which is what we call people who look after buildings, especially the hallways and doorways.

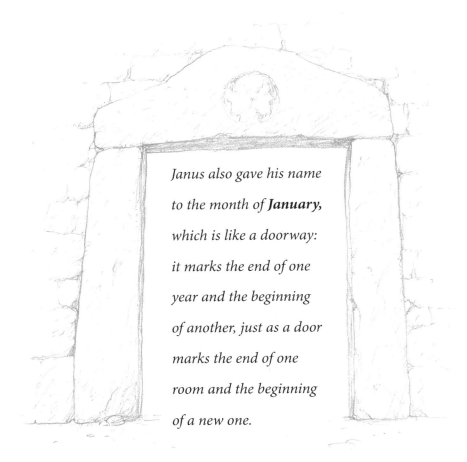

*Janus also gave his name to the month of **January,** which is like a doorway: it marks the end of one year and the beginning of another, just as a door marks the end of one room and the beginning of a new one.*

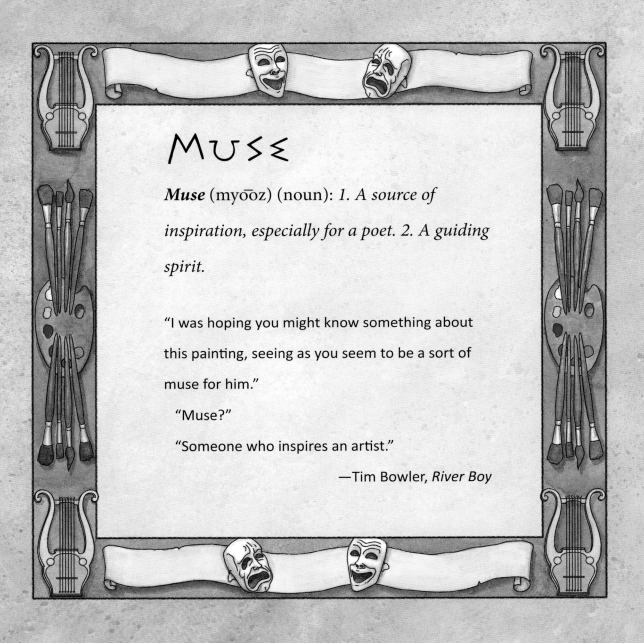

MUSE

Muse (myo͞oz) (noun): *1. A source of inspiration, especially for a poet. 2. A guiding spirit.*

"I was hoping you might know something about this painting, seeing as you seem to be a sort of muse for him."

"Muse?"

"Someone who inspires an artist."

—Tim Bowler, *River Boy*

The nine **Muses** were daughters of Zeus, chief of the gods, and Mnemosyne, the goddess of memory. When they were small, their mother would gather the little girls around her feet and tell stories. Draping her long hair around them like a tent, she spun tales about the birth of the gods, the exploits of heroes and monsters, and all that had happened since the beginning of time.

The young goddesses loved the stories. As soon as they were big enough, they turned the tales into plays and poems, which they performed in front of the gods on Mount Olympus. For costumes, Selene, the goddess of the moon, gave them silver capes. Hera, the queen of the gods, lent them her peacock carriage, and Zeus even made them a copy of his thunderbolt. The gods loved these shows and clapped and laughed at the clever Muses.

Whether they performed comedy or tragedy, poetry or dance, the Muses always included song. When their best friend, Apollo, god of light and music, accompanied them on his lyre, the Muses' voices rang especially sweet and true. Their songs soared through the Halls of Mount Olympus, down the mountainside, and all the way to earth, where poets suddenly found the words they were searching for, artists painted with bolder strokes, and musicians felt the stirrings of new melodies.

Whenever they needed inspiration, artists on earth would pray to the Muses. And the Muses listened, singing words of encouragement in response. They are known to listen still, which is why even today artists call to them for help.

SING IN ME, MUSE, AND THROUGH ME TELL THE STORY...

*The Greeks built temples in honor of the nine Muses and called them **museums**. Today, **museums** house collections of art, science, and history—work that the Muses inspired, and work that inspires us today.*

*Because of their wonderful voices, the Muses have also given us the words **music** and **musical**.*

NEMESIS

Nemesis (nĕm′ĭ-sĭs) (noun): *1. A source of harm or ruin. 2. An opponent that cannot be beaten or overcome. 3. One that inflicts retribution or vengeance.*

The children were alone with their nemesis, a word which here means, "The worst enemy you could imagine."

—Lemony Snicket, *The Reptile Room*

Nemesis was the goddess of justice. Her job was to punish people guilty of evil deeds or of breaking the rules for good behavior. But she also made sure that nobody was too happy, and so she watched Fortuna like a hawk. If Nemesis thought Fortuna had given someone too much good luck, she became annoyed. Beating her wings furiously, she picked up her sword and whip and swooped down to earth to dispense bad luck and even things out. She especially punished people who became too full of pride because of their good fortune.

Once, an exceedingly rich king named Croesus received a visit from a wise man named Solon. Croesus insisted that Solon stay at his palace and installed him in a sumptuous apartment. He then took Solon to see his storerooms, which were overflowing with gold and magnificent treasures. Finally, after days of parading his wealth, Croesus posed Solon a question.

To the rich king's great annoyance, Solon the wise man did not name Croesus. Irritated, Croesus insisted, "Look at the luxury I live in. Look at my wealth. I am the richest man in the world. Surely I must be among the happiest."

But Solon gently shook his head and said, "Count no man happy till his death."

Croesus would soon learn the wisdom of Solon's words. Nemesis had overheard the conversation and was provoked by Croesus's pride. She decided to punish him. In time both Croesus's wife and oldest son died. He lost his entire kingdom in a dreadful war and became a miserable, unhappy man until his death.

Did Nemesis go too far? Some people thought so. Often, she punished people harshly for small transgressions. "The executioner of braggarts," the Greeks called her, and they spat on their own chests to avert her jealousy.

Not surprisingly, people began to associate Nemesis with misfortune and to dislike her. That's why Nemesis's name has become a word we use to describe an unbeatable foe or the source of one's ruin.

If you hear someone say, **"He's as rich as Croesus,"** it means that a person is exceptionally wealthy. This expression comes from king Croesus (krē′səs) in this story. He lived from 560 to 546 BCE in Lydia, which is in present-day Turkey.

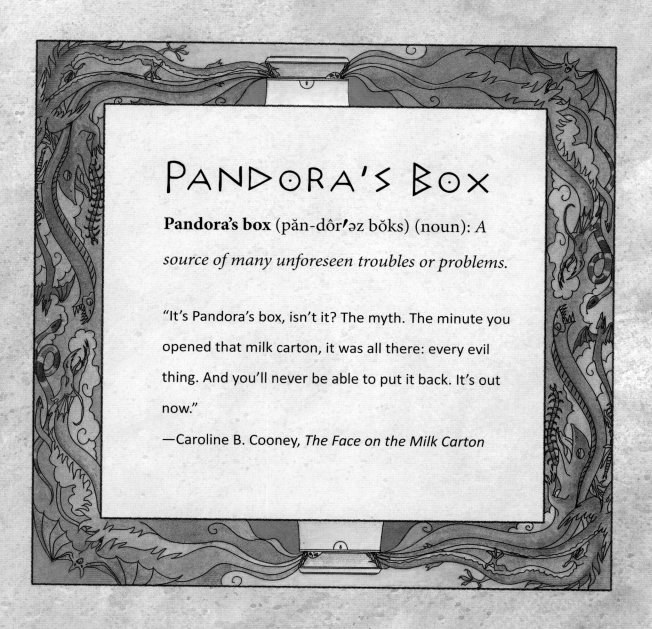

PANDORA'S BOX

Pandora's box (păn-dôr′əz bŏks) (noun): *A source of many unforeseen troubles or problems.*

"It's Pandora's box, isn't it? The myth. The minute you opened that milk carton, it was all there: every evil thing. And you'll never be able to put it back. It's out now."

—Caroline B. Cooney, *The Face on the Milk Carton*

Pandora was the first woman on earth. Zeus commanded Hephaestus, the god of fire and sculpture, to create her. Hephaestus modeled her body of earth, gave her a face like the immortal goddesses, and infused her with a human voice and vigor.

When he was done, each god bestowed a special gift on her. Aphrodite gave her matchless beauty. Athena clothed her in silken gowns and taught her the art of needlework. Apollo gave her the gift of music, Hermes the power of persuasion. The three Graces covered her in jewels and braided her hair with sweetly scented flowers. When the gods and goddesses were finished, Zeus gave her one final gift: insatiable curiosity.

Because they had granted her one gift each, the gods named this new creature Pandora, which means "all-gifts."

But Zeus had not made Pandora out of kindness. Rather, he was planning to use her as a way to punish humans and their protector the god Prometheus. Prometheus had stolen fire from the gods in defiance of Zeus's orders and given it to mankind. Knowing that Prometheus would be suspicious of a gift from him, Zeus offered Pandora in marriage to Epimetheus, who was Prometheus's brother. As a wedding gift he sent along a lovely carved box. Handing the box to Pandora, Zeus looked her in the eye and warned, "Don't ever open it."

In those days the world was a wonderful place to live. There was no sadness, no sickness, no old age, and no quarrels, and Pandora was very happy. Only one thing came to bother her: the mysterious box and its forbidden content.

She could not get the box out of her mind. *Why give a wedding gift and tell me I cannot open it? Surely Zeus had not meant what he said,* thought Pandora.

One day while Epimetheus was away, Pandora could no longer resist the urge to sneak a look inside the box. Carefully she cracked the lid open. Something within was crawling around.

Tiny voices pleaded with her to let them out. Overcome with curiosity, Pandora flung open the lid.

LET US OUT, LET US OUT!

Out from the box flew howling, wailing, snarling, insectlike creatures. Every misery burst forth: disease, anger, cruelty, old age, despair, pain, suffering, lies, envy, gossip, vanity, greed, anxiety, and revenge filled the room and flew out the window to scatter all over the world.

Horrified, Pandora slammed the lid shut. She tried to catch some of the miseries and put them back into the box, but it was too late. The only thing left in the box was a small, trembling thing—hope.

From then on, human life has been filled with great difficulty. But because Pandora caught hope before it could escape, humans are able to endure all the hardships that afflict us. With hope, all things are possible.

The Romans called Hephaestus, the god that made Pandora out of clay, Vulcan. The god of fire, he lived inside Mount Etna, where he constantly labored at his forge, fashioning tools, jewelry, and even robots. Sometimes he worked so hard that his forge overheated, causing Mount Etna to burst forth with black smoke and fire, sending melted rocks down the mountainside. Because it was Vulcan who brought about these eruptions, people began to call Mount Etna and every mountain that behaved similarly a **volcano.**

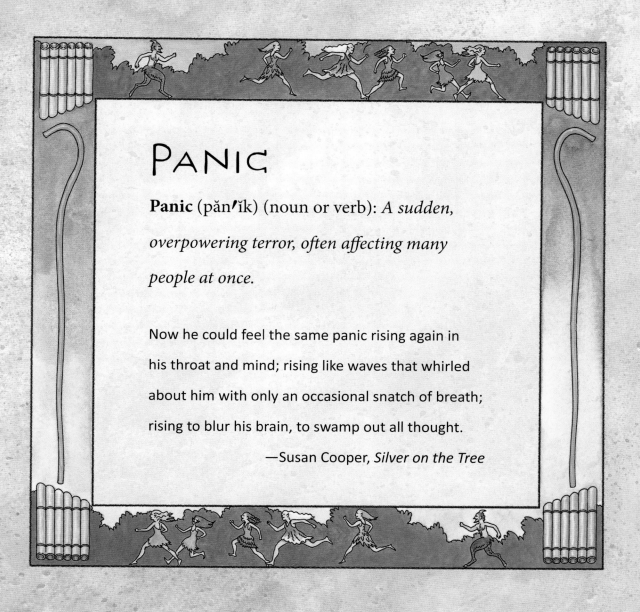

Panic

Panic (păn′ĭk) (noun or verb): *A sudden, overpowering terror, often affecting many people at once.*

Now he could feel the same panic rising again in his throat and mind; rising like waves that whirled about him with only an occasional snatch of breath; rising to blur his brain, to swamp out all thought.

—Susan Cooper, *Silver on the Tree*

Pan, the god of flocks and shepherds, was a happy-go-lucky fellow. With legs like a goat, horns on his head, and a little beard, Pan looked half human, half goat. He roamed around the woodlands, taking care of the sheep, the goats, and the cows. In his spare time, he played with the nymphs and other woodland creatures. Mostly, Pan enjoyed his carefree life—except when he fell in love with one of the nymphs. Whenever he tried to steal a kiss, they pushed him away. To them, his goatlike face was frightening.

One day, after yet another rejection, Pan slunk away into the deepest recesses of the forest and sulked for a long time. Finally, he grew tired of his own moping and decided the only thing that could cheer him up was playing a prank. Pan loved mischief.

Hiding in a clump of bushes along a forest road, he waited quietly. Soon he heard the tap-tapping of an approaching traveler. As the poor man walked by, Pan jumped up from his hiding place and let out a bloodcurdling cry.

The traveler became so terrified that his mouth dried up, his heart raced, and he sprinted wildly off as fast as his legs would carry him.

Pan laughed and laughed at the sight of the fleeing fellow and decided to play that trick each time he needed cheering up. Ever since, the feeling Pan created in the traveler is called *panic* because it was he who first inspired it.

*Pan once fell in love with a nymph who escaped from him by running down a riverbank and turning herself into a reed. Pan searched all along the river but never found her. To console himself, he cut down several hollow reeds and fashioned them into a musical instrument, which to this day we call a **pan flute**.*

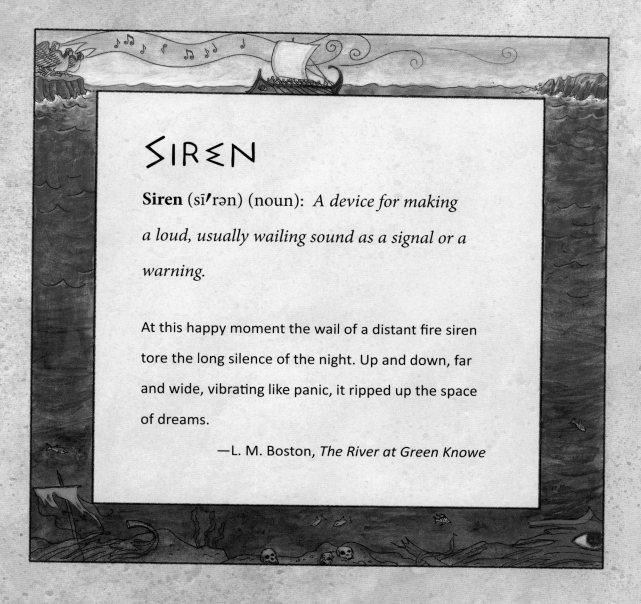

Siren

Siren (sī′rən) (noun): *A device for making a loud, usually wailing sound as a signal or a warning.*

At this happy moment the wail of a distant fire siren tore the long silence of the night. Up and down, far and wide, vibrating like panic, it ripped up the space of dreams.

—L. M. Boston, *The River at Green Knowe*

The **Sirens** were deities, minor goddesses, famous for their musical talents. They were half-bird, half-female creatures that sang in the most heavenly voices. Gods and mortals alike heaped praise on them, and as sometimes happens, all that praise made them vain.

One day, while the Sirens were visiting Mount Olympus, the Muses put on an especially enchanting performance. Applauding enthusiastically, the gods declared the performance unsurpassable. Hera, feeling impish, leaned over and whispered to the Sirens, "If you challenge the Muses to a singing competition, I am certain your voices will be declared superior."

Fluffing their feathers with undisguised pride, the Sirens did challenge the Muses to a contest, and their singing was lovely indeed. Still, when the Muses took the stage, their voices were so beautiful that the wind itself stopped to listen and the gods immediately declared them the winners. Then Zeus demanded that the Sirens pluck enough feathers from their bodies for each Muse to make a crown for herself.

Enraged, the Sirens fled and hid among the jagged rocks and sharp cliffs along the coast. In that forsaken and bitter landscape, their humiliation turned them into vengeful monsters. Instead of singing to create beauty, they began to use their bewitching voices to lure sailors to the shores, where the men were dashed to death on the treacherous cliffs.

And so, even though the Sirens' song was still beautiful, it began to signal danger. If anyone came close enough to hear the Sirens, they should stay away, and that is the how we use the word *siren* to this very day.

*A woman who is considered very attractive but treacherous is sometimes called a **siren**. And a **siren song** means a dangerous, beautiful call you can't resist.*

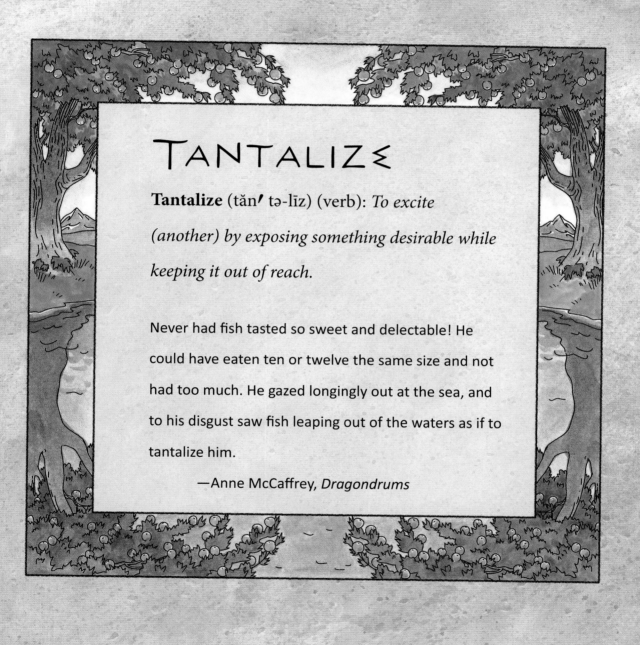

TANTALIZE

Tantalize (tăn′ tə-līz) (verb): *To excite (another) by exposing something desirable while keeping it out of reach.*

Never had fish tasted so sweet and delectable! He could have eaten ten or twelve the same size and not had too much. He gazed longingly out at the sea, and to his disgust saw fish leaping out of the waters as if to tantalize him.

—Anne McCaffrey, *Dragondrums*

Tantalus was the human son of Zeus and the nymph Plouto. He was a great favorite among all the gods and was even invited to dine at Mount Olympus. This so filled him with self-importance that he did a very wicked thing. He invited the gods to a banquet at his house and had his own son, Pelops, cooked up and served as a meal. Nobody knows why he did such a dreadful thing, but it infuriated the gods—especially Zeus.

First, Zeus restored poor Pelops to life. Then he turned to Tantalus, picked him up, and threw him into the deepest, darkest part of the underworld. But that was not enough. To really punish Tantalus, Zeus stuck him in a pool with water reaching up to his neck. Every time Tantalus bent to get a drink, the water sank out of reach. Around the pool grew trees laden with fruits, but whenever Tantalus reached out to pick an apple or a peach, the wind blew the branches away. Tantalus was condemned to be surrounded by food and water yet remain hungry and thirsty for all time.

Tantalus was full of overbearing pride and arrogance, which in Greek is called **hubris** (hyoo′brĭs). The gods, especially Nemesis, always punished hubris.

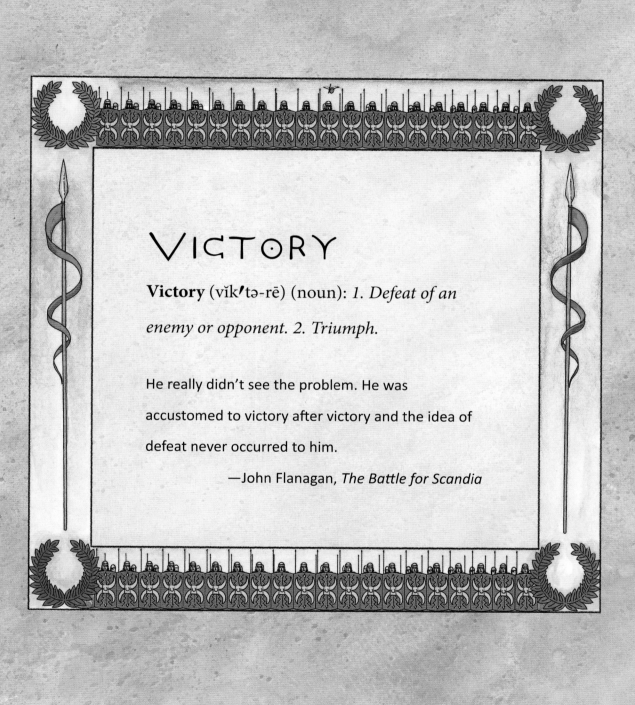

VICTORY

Victory (vĭk′tə-rē) (noun): *1. Defeat of an enemy or opponent. 2. Triumph.*

He really didn't see the problem. He was accustomed to victory after victory and the idea of defeat never occurred to him.

—John Flanagan, *The Battle for Scandia*

Even though the goddess **Victoria** was tiny, her power was immense.

Victoria always accompanied Minerva, the goddess of wisdom and war, and she was so little that she could fit into Minerva's hand. Sometimes, when Minerva was on her way to a battle, she would scoop up Victoria in her hand and carry her, but most of the time the little goddess sped along by herself, her wings beating so fast that they were nearly invisible.

As soon as she reached a battleground, Victoria set to work. First she flew to one side and listened in on the conversations of the generals and the soldiers. Then she hastened to the other side to hear their talk and reasons for war. Only when she fully understood who fought for a fair and just cause did she act. Then she quickly dove down and guided the horses and the spears of the men she championed, making sure they won.

Sometimes other gods and goddesses would become involved in war by helping their favorite heroes. They didn't care who was fighting for a just cause, so if Victoria was absent it was impossible to be certain which side would win. Only when Victoria was present at the battle would the righteous side be sure to triumph.

If Victoria was with them, the soldiers could always feel it. Their bodies grew stronger, their thinking became sharper, and their strategy improved. With her help a small army could conquer a larger one.

Upon returning from war, the triumphant generals and warriors always offered thanksgiving and sacrifices to tiny Victoria. And so, in time her name became synonymous with winning, and not just on the battlefield, but in every kind of competition.

*Victoria is the Roman name for the Greek goddess **Nike***
(nī′kē), and Minerva (mĭ-nŭr′və) is what they called the
Greek goddess Athena. The Greeks loved these two goddesses
so much that they named their capital city, Athens, after
Athena, and placed statues of Nike all along the city walls
to ensure their triumph in every battle and contest.

THE END

Author's Note

No mythology has given English as many words as the Greek and the Roman myths. To make this book accessible and dramatic, I have chosen to focus on words that have their origin in characters whose stories clearly illuminate why their names became words.

But many more words than those included here have their origin in classical mythology. The world of science is rich with them. *Titanium*, for instance, the strongest metal ever known, takes its name from the Titans, an ancient race of fiercely strong gods. Astronomy is likewise filled with the names of gods and goddesses. *Mercury, Venus, Mars, Jupiter, Saturn, Uranus, Neptune*, and *Pluto*, the names of the planets in our own solar system, are just a few.

If you broaden the scope to include not just words that come from characters but those from objects and places, there is an even larger catch. The word *lethal*, for instance, comes from the river Lethe, which flowed through Hades, the Greek underworld and the home of the dead. *Labyrinth* was first the name of a maze built to contain a monster called the Minotaur. The Greek word for star is *astron*, so *astronomy* means the study of the

THE MINOTAUR

positions and composition of stars. A dis-*aster* literally means to have the stars against you, and *asterisk* means "little star," which is why it shows up as this symbol * on your keyboard.

Sooner or later all students of mythology ask, "Is that a Greek god or a Roman one?" The reason for the confusion is this: About two thousand years ago, the Romans conquered the Greeks, heard their myths, and were spellbound. When they translated the stories from Greek into their own language, Latin, they often gave the gods and goddesses new names. For example, the Greeks called the chief of the gods Zeus, but the Romans named him Jupiter and even called him Jove from time to time. Because people felt that to be born under the protection of Jove would make you content and happy, Jove has given us the word *jovial,* which means "cheerful."

ZEUS

In some cases the Latin names traveled into English; other times the Greek did. And occasionally, both versions of the name have become words. The Greek goddess of cleanliness and good health, Hygeia, has given us the word *hygiene,* which we use to describe good, healthful behav-

iors. The Romans called this goddess Salus, and her name, too, survives in English. As they greeted one another, the Romans called out, "Salus!" meaning "How is your health?" Today we call a greeting a *salute,* and thus remember the goddess of good health without even realizing it.

"SALUS!"

THE ROMAN SALUTE

What is important isn't whether the word is from Greek or Latin, but that the characters and their stories so captured people's imaginations that their names live on today, thousands of years after their stories were first told. To avoid confusion, I have used Latin names for the characters in the stories when the word in question came into English via Latin, and Greek names when the word came directly from the Greek. This is why Athena has her Greek name in the story about Arachne, but I use her Latin name in the story about Victoria.

CORRESPONDENCES

GREEK	LATIN
Achilles (ə-kĭl′ēz)	Achilles
Aphrodite (ăf′rə-dī′tē)	Venus (vē′nəs)
Apollo (ə-pŏl′ō)	Apollo
Arachne (ə-răk′nē)	Arachne
Athena (ə-thē′nə)	Minerva (mĭ-nŭr′və)
Atropos (ăt′-rə-pōs′)	Morta (môr′tə)
Charites (kār′ĭ-təs)	Gratiae (grā′shē′ə)
Clotho (klō′thō)	Nona (nō′nə)
Daemon (dī′mōn)	Genius (jēn′yəs)
Echo (ĕk′ō)	Echo
Ephimetheus (ĕp′ə-mē′thē-əs)	Epimetheus
Erinyes (ĭ-rĭn′ē-ez)	Furiae (fyŏŏr′ē-ə) /the Furies
Hephaestus (hĭ-fĕs′təs)	Vulcan (vŭl′kən)
Hera (hîr′ə)	Juno (jōō′nō)
Hygeia (hī-jē′ə)	Salus (sälōōs)
Hypnos (hĭp-nŏs)	Somnus (sŏm′nəs)
	Janus (jā′nəs)
Lachesis (lăk′ĭ-sĭs)	Decuma (dē′kōō′mə)
Mnemosyne (nĭ-mŏs′ə-nē)	Moneta (mō′nā′tá)
Moirai (moi′rāy)	Fata (fá′tá)/the Fates
Mousai (mōō′sā)	Muses (myōō′zəs)
Narcissus (när-sĭs′əs)	Narcissus
Nemesis (nĕm′ĭ-sĭs)	Invidia (ĭn-vĭd′ē′ə), Rivalitas
Nike (nī′kē)	Victoria (vĭk-tōr′ē-ə)
Nyx (nĭks)	Nox (nŏks)
Pan (păn)	Faunus (fŏ′nəs)
Pandora (păn-dôr′ə)	Pandora
Prometheus (prə-mē′thē-əs)	Prometheus
Selene (sə-lē′nē)	Luna (lōō′nə)
Siren (sī′rən)	Siren
Tantalus (tăn′tə-ləs)	Tantalus
Thalia (thə-lī′ə)	Thalia
Tyche (tĭ′kē)	Fortuna (fôr′tōō′nə)
Zeus (zōōs)	Jupiter/Jove (jōō′pĭ-tər) (jōv)

DEFINITION

Greek hero.

Goddess of beauty and love.

God of light and musk.

Skilled weaver who was turned into a spider.

Goddess of wisdom and war, patron goddess of the arts.

Eldest of three Fates, cut thread of life.

Goddess of beauty and charm.

Youngest of three Fates, spun thread of life.

Personal spirit.

Nymph.

The titan god of afterthought.

Goddesses of retribution and vengeance.

God of fire, blacksmiths, sculpture.

Queen of the gods, goddess of marriage, family.

Goddess of good health.

God of sleep.

God of door and halls, beginnings and endings.

Middle of three Fates, measured thread of life.

Goddess of memory, mother of the Muses.

The three goddesses of destiny.

Goddesses of the arts.

Greek youth who fell in love with himself.

Goddess of justice and retribution.

Goddess of victory.

Goddess of the night.

God of flocks and shepherds.

The first woman.

The titan god of forethought and clever counsel.

Goddess of the moon.

Part bird, part female deity.

Mortal son of Zeus.

Youngest of the Graces.

Goddess of good fortune.

Chief among the gods.

SELENE / LUNA

SELECTED BIBLIOGRAPHY

The American Heritage Dictionary, fourth edition. Boston: Houghton Mifflin, 2001.

Asimov, Isaac. *Words from the Myths*. Boston: Houghton Mifflin, 1961.

Bulfinch, Thomas. *The Age of Fable*. Philadelphia: Running Press, 1990.

———. *Bulfinch's Mythology*. New York: Modern Library, 1998.

Cotterell, Arthur. *The Macmillan Illustrated Encyclopedia of Myths and Legends*. New York: Macmillan, 1989.

D'Aulaire, Ingri, and Edgar Parin. *D'Aulaires' Book of Greek Myths*. New York: Doubleday, 1962.

Graves, Robert. *Greek Gods and Heroes*. New York: Bantam, Doubleday, 2001.

———. *The Greek Myths: Gods, Goddesses and Mythology*. Tarrytown, N.Y.: Marshall Cavendish, 2005.

Hamilton, Edith. *Mythology*. Boston: Little, Brown, 1942.

Hamilton, Robert. *The Facts on File Encyclopedia of Word and Phrase Origins*. New York: Checkmark Books, 1997.

Hesiod, *Theogony Works and Days*. Translated by M. L. West. Oxford: Oxford University Press, 1999.

Hicks, Peter. *Gods and Goddesses in the Daily Life of the Ancient Romans*. Columbus, Ohio: McGraw Hill Children's Publishing, 2003.

Homer, *The Iliad*. Translated by Robert Fagles. New York: Penguin Classics, 1990.

Kravitz, David. *Who's Who in Greek and Roman Mythology*. New York: Charles N. Potter, 1975.

Limburg, Peter R. *Stories Behind Words*. New York: H. W. Wilson, 1986.

Low, Alice. *Greek Gods and Heroes*. New York: Aladdin Books, MacMillan, 1985.

McCaughrean, Geraldine. *Greek Myths*. New York: Margaret K. McElderry Books, 1993.

Morford, Mark P. O., and Robert J. Lenardon. *Classical Mythology*. New York: Oxford University Press, 2007.

Ovid, *Metamorphoses*. Translated by Charles Martin. New York: W. W. Norton, 2005.

Oxford English Dictionary, prepared by J. A. Simpson and E. S. C. Weiner. Oxford: Oxford University Press, 1991.

Philip, Neil. *Myths and Legends*. New York: DK Publishing, 1999.

Room, Alexander. *National Textbook Company's Classical Dictionary: The Origins of the Names of Characters in Classical Mythology and Literature*. Chicago: National Textbook Company, 1992.

Onions, C. T. *The Oxford Dictionary of English Etymology*. Oxford: Claredon Press, 1966.

Russell, William F. *Classic Myths to Read Aloud*. New York: Crown Publishers, 1989.

Smith, William, ed. *The Dictionary of Greek and Roman Biography and Mythology*. Boston: Little, Brown, 1867.

Switzer, Ellen, and Costas. *Gods, Heroes, and Monsters: Their Sources, Their Stories, and Their Meanings*. New York: Atheneum, 1988.

Woodcock, P. G. *Short Dictionary of Mythology*. New York: Philosophical Library, 1953.

Word Histories and Mysteries, from Quiche to Humble Pie. Boston: Houghton Mifflin, 1986.

Wyld, Henry Cecil. *The Universal Dictionary of the English Language*. London: Waverly Book Company, 1957.

WEB SOURCES

blog.oup.com/category/reference/Oxford_etymologist (Anatoly Liberman)

www.theoi.com

www.wordsources.info

www.wordinfo.info

ACKNOWLEDGMENTS

The author wishes to thank and acknowledge the following:

Dr. Eve Browning, professor of ancient Greek philosophy and classics at the University of Minnesota, Duluth, for her careful reading of the manuscript, insightful comments, and delightful conversation, and for ensuring the accuracy of the content.

Dr. Anatoly Liberman, professor of Germanic Studies and Linguistics at the University of Minnesota, and the man (actually, the genius) behind the blog The Oxford Etymologist, for keeping me linguistically exact.

Joe Pickett, executive editor of *The American Heritage Dictionaries,* for his invaluable help with finding quotes and teaching me to navigate advanced book searches.

Kristin Palm and her fourth grade students, the Hoffman kids, the Derauf kids, and all their friends, who listened to these word stories in their many incarnations.

My husband, Steve, for countless hours of listening and unwavering support.

My incomparable editor, Ann Rider, the muse of children's literature, whose questions, comments, and faith in the project kept me on my toes and kept me going when other muses fell silent.

ARTIST NOTES

On page 33, Leonardo da Vinci (the quintessential genius) is shown painting the Mona Lisa. The quote on page 51 is the opening line of Homer's epic poem the *Odyssey* (as translated by Robert Fitzgerald), and is probably the most famous invocation of the Muses in art or literature. Also depicted on this page are Shakespeare writing and Georgio Vasari painting arguably his greatest work: the *Last Judgment* fresco on the ceiling of the great cathedral Il Duomo of Florence. This cathedral features the largest brick dome ever constructed, and the figures in the fresco are monumental in scale.

The museum depicted on page 52 is the National Archaeological Museum of Athens.

The poses of Victoria/Nike on pages 80 and 82 are based on several well-known sculptures, including the *Winged Victory of Samothrace* (housed in the Louvre Museum in Paris), and the large outdoor Nike sculptures in Rhodes and Berlin. She is holding the laurel wreath that symbolizes victory.

INDEX

Achilles, 2–5
Achilles' heel, 1, 5
Amaltheia, 26
Aphrodite, 60
Apollo, 51, 60
Arachne, 8–12
arachnid, 7
arachnophobia, 12
asterisk, 84
astron, 84
astronomy, 84
Athena, 8–12, 60, 82
Atropos, 21, 22

Clotho, 20–21
cornucopia, 26
Croesus, 55–56, 58

daemon, 34
demon, 34
disaster, 84

Echo, 14–18
echo, 13

fate, 19, 21
Fates, the, 20–21
Fortuna, 24–26, 54
fortune, 23
Furies, the, 28–29
furious, 30
furor, 30
fury, 27

Genius, 32–33
genius, 31
grace, 35
graceful, 38
Graces, the, 36–38, 60
gracious, 38
grateful, 38
Gratia, 38
gratitude, 38

Hades, 84
Hephaestus, 60, 64
Hera, 14–15, 41, 43, 50, 73
Hermes, 60

heroes, 6
hubris, 78
Hygeia, 85
hygiene, 85
Hypnos, 40–43
hypnosis, 44
hypnotize, 39, 43

immortal, 22
infuriate, 30
insomnia, 44

janitor, 45, 47
January, 48
Janus, 46–48
Jove, 85
jovial, 85
Jupiter, 84

Labyrinth, 84
Lachesis, 21
lethal, 84
Lethe, 84

Mars, 84
Mercury, 84
Minerva, 80, 82
Minotaur, 84
Mnemosyne, 50
Morta, 22
mortal, 22
mortality, 22
Mount Olympus, 9, 14, 50, 51, 73, 76
muse, 49
Muses, the, 50–52, 73
museum, 52
music, 52
musical, 52

narcissism, 18
narcissist, 18
Narcissus, 16–18
Nemesis, 54–57, 78
nemesis, 53, 57
Neptune, 84
Nike, 82
nymph, 2, 6, 14, 15, 66, 70, 76
Nyx, 40

Pan, 66–70
Pandora, 60–64
Pandora's box, 59
pan flute, 70
panic, 65, 69
Pelops, 76–77
Pluto, 84
Prometheus, 61

Salus, 85
salute, 85
Saturn, 84
Selene, 50
siren, 71, 74
Sirens, the, 72–74
siren song, 74
Skedasos, 29
Solon, 55–56
Somnus, 44
stamen, 20, 22
stamina, 21, 22
Styx, the river, 2

tantalize, 75
Tantalus, 76–78
Tartarus, 28
Thalia, 41–42
titanium, 84
Titans, the, 84
Trojans, 5, 41, 43
Trojan War, 41–43

Uranus, 84

Venus, 37–38, 84
Victoria, 80–82
victory, 79
volcano, 64
Vulcan, 64

Zeus, 14–15, 26, 41–43, 50, 60–62, 73, 76–77, 85

EAU CLAIRE DISTRICT LIBRARY